Dad parks himself on the end of my bed and hands me the envelope. I tear it open, but then I have to take a moment to hold the letter against my chest and brace myself to deal with whatever it says. I feel the speeded-up thud of my heart and my hands shake as I unfold it. A single sheet of paper and one line – 'Thank you for your application' – then a short, straight-to-the-point sentence that is the next step on the way to achieving my dream – or total heartbreak.

I hear myself gasp, but I can't force any words out of my mouth. Dad tugs the letter from my clenched fists so he can read it himself.

'Sweetheart!' he murmurs, scanning the page.

'Good news?' says Mum from the doorway. 'Is it good news?'

Also available in the Sugar and Spice series:

SKIN DEEP

Also written by Malaika Rose Stanley and published
by Tamarind Books:

SPIKE AND ALI ENSON
SPIKE IN SPACE

Picture books for younger readers:

BABY RUBY BAWLED
MISS BUBBLE'S TROUBLES

A Sugar and Spice Novel

Dance Dreams

Malaika Rose Stanley

Illustrated by Sarah Coleman

Tamarind

DANCE DREAMS
A TAMARIND BOOK 978 1 848 53055 3

Published in Great Britain by Tamarind Books,
an imprint of Random House Children's Publishers UK
A Random House Group Company

This edition published 2013

1 3 5 7 9 10 8 6 4 2

Set in 12/16pt Minion Reg by Falcon Graphic Art Ltd

Tamarind Books are published by Random House Children's Publishers UK,
61–63 Uxbridge Road, London W5 5SA

www.**tamarindbooks**.co.uk
www.**randomhousechildrens**.co.uk
www.**randomhouse**.co.uk

Addresses for companies within The Random House Group Limited can be found at:
www.randomhouse.co.uk/offices.htm

THE RANDOM HOUSE GROUP Limited Reg. No. 954009

A CIP catalogue record for this book is available from the British Library.

Printed and bound in Great Britain by CPI Group (UK) Ltd, Croydon, CR0 4YY

For my sisters who are my best friends,
and for my best friends who are my sisters

1

Tip Top

It's the most important day of my entire life and I'm standing here, practically naked. OK, so I'm wearing my lucky lilac leotard, but there's not that much difference when you're being prodded and poked.

The woman walks around me in a circle, looking me up and down from every angle. She peers at the arches of my feet. She examines my ever-so-slightly knobbly knees and the symmetry of my hips. She inspects the curve of my lower back, the straightness of my spine and the perfect posture of my head and neck.

She reaches out to squeeze my wrists as if she's checking whether I'm fat enough to eat, and I shiver and let out a little scream.

'Oops, sorry,' she says. She smiles and rubs her

palms together. 'You know what they say, though, don't you? Cold hands, warm heart.'

I've heard that before, of course – from my mum and from my dance teacher. But Miss Lucas is a physiotherapist, and in her case I'm not sure it's true, because the torture is far from over.

'Take a seat, Keisha,' she says, reaching for her clipboard and scribbling some notes.

I'm here at the Birchwood School for Dance for a group audition – *the* audition – but the whole process starts with an individual assessment of our posture, flexibility and strength. I'm the last person to be seen.

'What other dance styles have you learned?' asks Miss Lucas. 'How old were you when you started *en pointe*?'

'Contemporary and a bit of tap,' I tell her. 'But I've been concentrating on ballet and I've been *en pointe* since last year.'

'OK, let's move on to your medical history,' she says. 'Do you take any regular medication? Do you have a physical disability? Any learning difficulties? Eating disorders? Have you ever been ill with asthma? Diabetes? Epilepsy? Arthritis?'

I fill in the gaps with a quick shake of my head,

and I feel more and more anxious as I listen to the long list of terrible things that could go wrong with my brain and body and put a stop to my dancing career before it's even begun.

'Have your periods started yet?' says Miss Lucas, bringing the interrogation to a close with her last, killer questions. 'Are they regular?'

I feel my face flush with embarrassment.

'Yes,' I mutter, looking at my feet.

'OK, let's have you lying down now,' she says, whipping her tape measure back out.

She's already made a note of my height, weight and shoe size, but now I have to bend my knees and raise my hips while she compares my legs – in millimetres! – to make sure they're exactly the same length. She assesses my hip rotation, lower back mobility, hamstring length, the flexibility of my knees, calves and ankles, and my abdominal strength and stability. She feels along the bones in my feet, which tickles, and I have to grit my teeth to stop myself squirming and giggling as she checks for any bony lumps and bumps.

Finally, I stand up again while she checks out my shoulder rotation – and then bends my hands back towards my arms to test the flexibility of my wrists. Ouch! Ouch! I'd been expecting the physio assessment, but no one had warned me how much it might hurt. Miss Lucas isn't exactly gentle, and she's definitely not leaving anything to chance.

'Nice to meet you, Keisha,' she says as she scrawls her signature at the bottom of the form. 'Everything looks tip-top.'

2

The Audition

I rush away from the physio suite towards the changing rooms, where I yank my boots back off and pull on my ballet shoes. My nerves are stretched tighter than a spandex tutu on a hippo. The atmosphere in the room is jittery. There are about twenty-five of us altogether. Most of the girls are quite a bit younger than me – obviously moving up from primary school and auditioning for a Year Seven place – and wearing pristine leotards and tights under their shrugs and Uggs. They are chatting to each other in high-pitched, over-excited voices, trying to disguise the worry and stress – and in some cases, pure terror – that is etched across their faces.

But it's the small group of older girls, competing for a Year Eight or Nine place like me, that I have to worry about, and as I pin my audition number to the front of my leotard my eyes automatically seek them out. These girls look like proper dancers, and they are the ones I'm up against. They are warming up, circling their necks and ankles, and bending and stretching their bodies like cheese strings. It's clear that most of them have been dancing since before they could walk. Their faces are full of intense concentration.

I glance in the mirror to check that my hair is perfectly scraped back and my bun is still in place, and I see the same steely look of determination on my own face. I try to put the other girls out of my mind. I tell myself to focus on my own performance and to stay strong and positive.

'Get ready, everyone!' shouts Miss Pritchard, who is co-ordinating the auditions.

I shake off my over-sized fleece and baggy ankle-warmers and tug at the neckline of my leotard as she herds us into the dance studio – like lambs to the slaughter.

'I want you all to relax and have fun,' says Miss Pritchard.

I gape at her. She's kidding, right?

'We will just be doing an ordinary, basic class,' she continues. 'There's nothing for you to worry about except that lot.' She waves a long, slender hand towards the beady-eyed panel sitting at the end of the room behind their clipboards, getting ready to watch our every move. Like wolves, I think.

'They don't bite – not hard, at any rate,' says Miss Pritchard, bubbling with laughter at her own joke. 'Remember, we are looking for potential and quality of movement, not perfect technique.'

We line up at the *barre* and I listen intently to her instructions. We move in perfect synchronicity to the steady plink-plonk of the piano, first bending our knees into slow, gentle *pliés*, and then flexing, pointing and arching our feet as we practise *tendus* and *dégagés*.

After each exercise, we turn round so that we can warm up both sides of our bodies, and we gradually move on to bigger, faster movements, circling and swinging our legs in *ronde de jambes* and *grand battements* to stretch our legs and loosen our hips.

'Pull up on your thighs,' says Miss Pritchard to the lad in front of me – one of only four boys who have joined us in the studio. 'Keep your head straight and front.'

I turn out my own leg and lengthen my neck and wait for her to correct me, but after watching for a few moments she moves on down the line. I don't know whether that is a good or a bad thing, but by the time we move into the centre of the studio for the second part of the class, I stop worrying about it.

All my attention is focused on my body. I strain to keep my hips square and my back pulled up. I feel the tug and stretch of the muscles in my thighs and the tendons in my calves as I extend my leg backwards and up high into *arabesque*. I arch my foot and straighten and point my toes. I hold my weight over my supporting leg for balance and then slowly – elegantly – raise my arms for extra control. With every movement, I feel the energy of the other dancers around me – like flashes of lightning – and it encourages and inspires me to leap higher and spin faster.

The class lasts just over an hour and we finish with the usual *révérence* – a special curtsey or bow to say thank you to the teacher and the pianist. I am panting for breath and my brown skin is slick and shiny with sweat, but somehow I have managed to follow Miss Pritchard's advice and I have actually enjoyed the whole experience.

I find Mum and Dad waiting for me in the entrance hall.

'How was it, honey?' says Dad. He takes my holdall in one hand and squeezes my shoulder with the other. 'How did you get on?'

'OK,' I say cautiously. 'I think it was OK.'

'Good girl,' says Mum. 'Well done. I bet you're relieved it's all over and you don't have to keep it a secret any longer.'

I bite my lip. It's ages since Birchwood sent the letter inviting me to a first audition. I feel terrible, but I still haven't breathed a word about it to any of my friends. I'm terrified of getting my hopes up in case my dream of attending Birchwood doesn't come true.

And if, by some miracle, it does, I know they are going to be really gutted about me moving schools. I'll really miss them too, and sometimes I wonder if I'll be able to survive without my besties by my side.

3

Secrets and Surprises

The next morning I meet my friends outside the Bhangra Balti House for the short walk to school. We are all dressed in the regulation Halsall High School uniform, but to be honest, we couldn't look more different:

I am wearing grey suede ballet flats and my blue pleated skirt is almost as short as a tutu.

As usual, Bee is sporting stretchy navy trousers teamed with black, high-top trainers.

Ebyan has a scarf over her head, and a slinky, long-sleeved grey cardigan with thumb holes draped over a stylish navy maxi skirt.

Destiny – my cousin – is wearing a grey beret pulled down over her curls and a tight-fitting navy blazer. Even though her stripy tie is properly knotted over her white shirt, which is buttoned up all the way to the top, she still manages to look cool.

Ebyan and Destiny swagger and strut as if they're on an international mid-summer designer fashion catwalk and not a chewing-gum-studded pavement on a grey February morning in Birmingham. They like to make an entrance, even if it is only through the school gates.

Bee and I trail them across the playground, jumping over the piles of bags, which Joel Daley-Clarke and a whole load of other Year Eight lads are using as goalposts. Joel grins and punches the air, although if I'm honest, I think that's more to do with his team scoring than because he's caught a glimpse of me. I wish it was because of that, though. Me and half the other girls in our year!

We walk on, picking our way through a gaggle of shrieking Year Sevens and side-stepping a coven of all-ages-welcome goths, through the deafening roar of hundreds of teenagers, all pushing and shoving, yelling and shouting. It's the last day before half term and everyone is excited about having a whole week of freedom and spending time with their mates.

I glance round at my own friends – at Destiny and my oldest bestie Ebyan – and then back at Bee, who smiles at me. She's the newest member of our group, and over the past few months, with our expert help, she has been transformed from freaky geek to sleek and chic. Last term, she and Destiny both entered the *Bright Sparks* talent and beauty competition. Destiny got through to the finals, but then a nerve in her face was zapped by a virus, which messed up her chances. She went through a really hard time, but we all stuck together and supported her.

I know I am lucky to have such good friends. We trust each other. We can tell each other everything – well, nearly everything. I still haven't mentioned yesterday's audition.

We make our way through the main entrance and along the crowded corridor to our lockers.

'Double maths,' groans Destiny. 'Shouldn't there be a law against that?'

'I think it's included in the Universal Declaration of Human Rights,' says Ebyan.

'Really?' says Destiny, before she realizes it's a joke.

'Don't worry,' says Bee mischievously. 'We've got double PE to look forward to after lunch.'

Now it's Ebyan's turn to grumble. 'I don't know why there's all this pressure for everyone to be sporty ever since Team GB ruled at the Olympics. It's all right for you two,' she says, looking at Bee and Destiny. 'You like getting all muddy and bruised!'

I laugh. She's right. Destiny likes football and Bee loves cross-country, but Ebyan would struggle to run from a burning building. As a dancer, I'm somewhere in the middle – and PE does mean we get to see Joel Daley-Clarke in his shorts.

'Are you feeling better now?' Bee asks me as she rummages through her locker.

I shrug my shoulders, not understanding.

'Yesterday,' she says. 'We thought you must be really ill. It was Valentine's Day.'

'Oh, no!' I say. 'I forgot all about it!' It's the truth, but it sounds lame even to me. I've always been into Valentine's Day – ever since I got a card with a frog on a heart-shaped lilypad from Elio Butera, before his family moved to Italy way back in Year Five. Not that it seems like I missed out on much this year. No one is exactly clamouring to tell me about getting any romantic cards, red roses or yummy chocolates – or any passionate declarations of undying love.

'Why weren't you in school, then?' says Bee. She frowns, confused. 'And why are you being so secretive?'

'I bet you have secrets sometimes too,' I say, avoiding her first question. 'Everyone does. Anyway, it's not a secret.' I laugh nervously. 'It's a surprise.'

Destiny pops a Mini-Mint and rolls her amber-coloured eyes.

'Ooh,' says Bee, pushing a loose strand of newly highlighted hair behind her ear. 'I love surprises.'

'Me too,' says Ebyan. She flutters her ultra-long eyelashes and peers at me from beneath her midnight-blue silk *hijab*. 'What is it?'

'If I tell you,' I begin, in a scary impersonation of a gangster, 'I'd have to—'

The buzzer sounds for registration. I am saved by the bell!

4

Half-Term Holiday

I've been going to classes at the Isabelle Kennedy Academy of Dance since I was seven or eight – every Saturday morning and two evenings a week after school. I wanted to go when I was even younger and I first saw *Angelina Ballerina* on the TV, but it took me ages to nag Mum and Dad into letting me have lessons because they said it cost too much money.

Dancing actually runs in my family, although you'd never know it from looking at my parents: Mum is a baby-catcher and Dad is a secret agent. OK, I admit it – half of that's a lie. Mum is really a community midwife, but Dad is a transport engineer.

It's Nan – Dad's mum – who is the dancer. We hardly ever see her because she lives in New York.

She's from Jamaica originally, but she moved to America when she was accepted into the Dance Theater of Harlem in the 1970s. She was one of the first Caribbean dancers to go on tour and perform in Russia and South Africa.

Occasionally, I talk to her on Skype and she tells me stories about her life as a professional dancer.

'We used to wear tan-coloured pantyhose and dye our shoes with *Caribbean Coffee* foundation,' she says. 'Dance tights and *pointe* shoes were only available in traditional pink and it looked odd to have a brown upper body with pink legs and feet.'

'Like a flamingo in reverse,' I suggest.

'Flamingos are seriously beautiful movers,' says Nan, making me laugh. 'It's true, sugar. You check them out on YouTube. They can balance on one leg for hours and their mating dance is awesome.' She stands up, moves back and shows me her flamingo impersonation – a perfect pirouette with her foot pulled up into the *retiré* position, followed by a sideways three-step *chassé* that I can't quite see because the angle of her webcam is too high. She sits down again and pats her chest, pretending to be old and out of breath. As if!

'We looked even pinker if the stage lighting had

a red base,' she says. 'Yellow lighting is much more flattering for the skin tones of black performers.'

I already knew about the pink feet problem. Mum had tried – and failed – to find ballet shoes that match my skin colour but I'd never heard about the problem with lighting before.

It was after I'd showed Nan a few of my own dance moves on Skype when I was little that she phoned Dad to tell him I had 'outstanding natural talent'. Of course, Dad wouldn't recognize natural talent if it leaped up in a *grand jeté* and bit him on the bum! But he did enrol me for lessons – and my teacher, Miss Fizz, soon agreed that I had 'genuine flair' and could go really far. Since then, she's even given me a few extra lessons, free of charge, to prepare for exams and festivals, for the Birmingham Royal Ballet associates programme and, most recently, for the Birchwood auditions. And it was Miss Fizz who told us about the Music and Dance Scheme, which is great because a scholarship would help Mum and Dad out with the fees.

Like Halsall High, the Kennedy Academy is closed for half term.

'Good!' Mum says. 'You've been totally obsessed

with dance for weeks. You need a break. Why don't you try something different?'

Apart from a few morning exercises – I think I'd die if I didn't start the day with some *pliés* and *tendus*, and no serious dancer can afford to miss a morning session, especially if there's the chance of another audition coming up – I decide to take her advice. I talk it over with my friends. The weather is rubbish – rainy and cold – and we're really strapped for cash because a certain someone has a birthday coming up soon, but we treat it as a challenge and somehow we manage to come up with something new for every single day of the half term.

Monday: Bee's mum is at the hairdresser's so we go round to her house and she sets up her living room for an aerobics class. She has enough T-shirts and cycling shorts to kit us all out properly and she's a bit bossy, but she seems to know what she's doing. Luckily, her brothers are all out, or they'd probably be poking their heads round the door and making jokes at our expense. It's weird, but even though we've known Bee for ages now and we often go round to her house, I've barely seen her older brothers. I met Hugo once, I remember, but mostly they're off out doing various sporty things. Or boy stuff.

'It's important to warm up,' Bee says now, making us march on the spot before building up to more vigorous skipping, leaping, hopping and lunging.

After about ten minutes, we are all puffing and panting. I'm fit from all my dancing, but by the end of the session I think I'm about to have a heart attack and Ebyan looks like she's already had one.

'No pain, no gain,' laughs Bee as we stagger to the sofa and collapse into a heap to recover.

She feels sorry for us, though. She makes popcorn, and we spend the afternoon singing along to old episodes of *Glee* on TV.

Tuesday: We walk to the Midlands Arts Centre to see an art exhibition.

'A bit of culture,' explains Destiny, but we're just glad she hasn't come up with anything too strenuous because we are still stiff and aching from yesterday.

The gallery is small, but it doesn't matter because so is the art. Every exhibit is postcard-sized. Each one is by a different artist, using different materials and styles – computer graphics, collages, photographs, oil paintings, charcoal sketches.

At the end of the exhibition, there are plain

postcards and art materials laid out so we can make our own work of art, to add to the public exhibition or take home.

'Why don't we do portraits of each other?' suggests Destiny.

Bee's picture makes me look like I belong on a Wanted poster – but I still pin it up on my bedroom wall.

Wednesday: We have a clothes swap at Ebyan's house. We gather up the clothes we never wear any more and put them in a big pile and take turns trying them on. We all end up with more new clothes than if we'd gone shopping – and they're free!

Ebyan's mum makes us lunch and then we borrow her sewing machine and Eb shows us how to recycle old jeans or trousers to make a bag.

'What are we going to do with the stuff no one wants?' asks Destiny, which we can all see is mainly Bee's sports gear.

'Charity shop,' says Ebyan.

It's perfect – new clothes, new bag and even a good deed for the day.

Thursday: This is my day and it's finally stopped

raining so now we've recovered from aerobics, we take my dog, Diesel, on a really long walk along the canal. At first, I don't think my friends are too impressed, even when I tell them I found out that Birmingham has more kilometres of canal than Venice.

'But no gondolas,' says Ebyan.

'And no ice cream,' says Destiny.

'And no hunky Italians,' says Bee.

It's hard to argue with that when all we can see is narrowboats and locks and anglers in caps. But we have a laugh and Diesel has a good time racing along the towpath – and we even find somewhere to buy a hot chocolate drink with whipped cream and sprinkles.

Friday: We come up with today's plan together. We go to the shopping centre and try to nab as much free stuff as we can – without stealing it! We eat cubes of cheese on sticks and we are given a small can of something low-calorie and fizzy by a bloke dressed as a can of something low-calorie and fizzy. We apply for store cards that we're not even old enough to use and get sprays and samples of expensive perfume. Destiny even scores a free make-over at the cosmetics counter.

'We can't afford to buy anything,' she admits. 'But I'll be modelling it for you. It'll be like free advertising.'

When we run out of places to scrounge from, we sit on a bench, chatting, talent-spotting and cracking up over nothing. It's the best half term ever. Just me and my BFFs. Who needs money when you have good mates?

But will I still have good friends if I tell them I'm trying to leave? Trying to go to a different school? Even if it is to follow my dreams . . .

5

Morning News

On Saturday morning, I am woken by Diesel snuffling
in my ear and I am instantly on high alert. He's not
usually allowed in the bedrooms, so I know he's
not alone. I turn over, and behind our bouncing,
floppy-eared, waggy-tailed hairy heap I catch a quick
glimpse of Dad.

'Time to find out if Birchwood are inviting you
back for a second audition,' he says, holding a white
envelope between his finger and thumb and pointing
at the embossed logo. He sounds nervous – nearly as
bad as I feel.

I sit up, and Diesel starts barking with excitement
and bounding backwards and forwards across the
room. Maybe he knows something we don't. Maybe
he knows it's good news.

Dad parks himself on the end of my bed and hands me the envelope. I tear it open, but then I have to take a moment to hold the letter against my chest and brace myself to deal with whatever it says. I feel the speeded-up thud of my heart and my hands shake as I unfold it. A single sheet of paper and one line – 'Thank you for your application' – then a short, straight-to-the-point sentence that is the next step on the way to achieving my dream – or total heartbreak.

I hear myself gasp, but I can't force any words out of my mouth. Dad tugs the letter from my clenched fists so he can read it himself.

'Sweetheart!' he murmurs, scanning the page.

'Good news?' says Mum from the doorway. 'Is it good news?' She comes into the room and reads the letter over Dad's shoulder, and a moment later we are all cheering and whooping and dancing around the room. Even Diesel joins the celebration, leaping up and down and wagging his tail.

I've been invited back to Birchwood for a second, individual audition!

'I have to phone Nan,' I say when we all get our breath back. 'Can I phone her?'

'OK,' says Dad. 'But later – it's only about four in

the morning there right now. And when you do, be quick. It's not free like Skype. It's expensive.'

Mum laughs and shakes her head at him. 'Take your time, love,' she says. 'Phone Destiny and your friends now if you like, though, but don't make yourself late for your dance class with Miss Fizz.'

I gulp. 'Mum . . .' I say slowly. 'Don't say anything to Aunty Dionne, will you? I, er, still haven't told Destiny or the others about the auditions. I don't want them to know until I know if it's going to work or not.' I screw up my face. 'It's just too *big*, somehow . . .' I tail off and see Mum and Dad exchanging glances.

It's clear they're not happy, but before they can say anything, I dive into my wardrobe to get my bag of dance gear. I can't wait to tell Miss Fizz I've got through to the second auditions!

Later, when I arrive at the Kennedy Academy and tell Miss Fizz I have a call-back, I see her green eyes flood with tears of pride and joy. She crushes me against her bony chest in a hug and I feel the razor-sharp edge of her collar bone digging into my cheek.

'I knew you'd do it,' she says as I try to wriggle away from the pain without her noticing. 'You'll sail through your solo audition.'

'I was thinking of a variation,' I say. 'I danced *La Esmeralda* at the festival last year. Maybe I should do that.'

'The school has already seen you perform classical ballet,' says Miss Fizz. 'Perhaps you could try something different.'

The Kennedy Academy teaches the complete A to Z of dance, from the Argentine tango to zumba and zydeco and everything in between, but I only take classes in a couple of them so I really hope she is thinking of one of those.

'But it's in three weeks!' I blurt out in a panic. 'There isn't time to do anything new.'

'Poppycock!' says Miss Fizz. 'A contemporary dance will demonstrate your versatility and showcase your strengths. You'll have to work hard, but I'll help with the choreography so you can concentrate on the dancing.'

I sigh with relief. At least she isn't expecting me to dance a drobushki or perform a paso doble, and at least she doesn't think I can prepare the solo all on my own.

'Over the weekend, I want you to choose a theme and find a piece of music,' she says.

'What? Like homework?' I ask, surprised. Miss Fizz

usually comes up with most of the ideas herself and we just get to dance.

She rips a bright yellow square of paper from her pad and jots down the details of an Internet site with music downloads for different styles of dance.

'Get cracking,' she says, sticking the Post-It note to my forehead. 'I'll see you for an extra lesson after school on Monday. Come at five, after the junior ballet, and we'll have an hour before the street-dance class.'

6

Gold and Silver

Getting cracking is harder than it sounds. All weekend, I keep hoping for a flash of inspiration, but by Monday lunch time I still haven't come up with anything I like. As usual, I'm sitting in the dining hall with Destiny, Ebyan and Keisha. Out of the corner of my eye, I see Joel Daley-Clarke messing about with his mates. Even from a distance it's hard not to stare at his seriously smouldering eyes and smooth, light-brown skin.

In my fave fantasy about him, I am walking home from school and it's pouring with rain. The light changes but when I look up, expecting to see the sun breaking out from behind the clouds, I see Joel Daley-Clarke holding a yellow umbrella above my head, shielding me from the rain while he himself is getting soaked. He is dripping wet and he looks like Elliot Knight summoning the rain in *Sinbad*. Joel lives in the opposite direction to me, but he holds my hand and offers to walk me home. I huddle up close to him under the brolly – and become totally delusional.

'Do you think I'm pretty?' I ask him – and he says no.

'Do you want to be with me for ever?' I ask – and he says no.

'If I were to leave, would you cry?' I ask – and he says no.

I walk away through the rain, squelching, with tears streaming down my face, but Joel Daley-Clarke reaches out and takes me in his arms.

'You're not pretty – you are *beautiful*,' he whispers. 'I don't want to be with you for ever. I *need* to be with you for ever. And no, I wouldn't cry if you walked away . . . I think I would die.'

The rain stops and a rainbow arches across the sky . . .

'Forget him,' says Bee, spotting the direction of my gaze and immediately deciphering the misty look in my eyes.

'Who?' I say automatically as I snap my head round to face her and jolt myself back to reality.

'Joel Daley-Clarke,' she says. 'I heard from Madison that he hooked up with someone on Valentine's Day.'

I feel my face flush and I glance at Destiny and Ebyan. Did they see me drooling over some other girl's boyfriend? But Ebyan is scribbling notes on a piece of paper, and Destiny is too busy picking the onions out of her veggie burger to notice anything. But like most of our year group, Destiny has a huge crush on Joel, especially after he came to see her playing the cello in the *Bright Sparks* competition last year. I bet she'll be really upset.

Luckily, Ebyan changes the subject away from boys. 'Have you chosen your project for Design and Technology yet?' she says, tapping her pen against her temple and looking thoughtful. 'I'm doing textiles. I found a place in town that sells cheap silk gauze and I'm going to experiment with different gold and silver dyes. I've already made a few notes.'

Ebyan is the original *hijabista* so it's not exactly a surprise. Her mum owns a Somali wedding shop called Suuqa Samiira and Eb's ambition is to be an eco-fashion designer and make trendy Islamic clothes.

'That sounds awesome,' Bee says. 'I'm thinking of

doing resistant materials.' She nudges Destiny's arm. 'What about you?'

'Food,' says Destiny. 'Definitely food.' She grins and takes another big bite of her burger.

I shrug. I haven't got a clue. DT – and anything else to do with school – has been the last thing on my mind. My mind is full of dance, but as I listen to Ebyan enthuse about patterns and colours and fabrics, I suddenly have a brilliant idea . . .

7

Fire and Water

Gold and silver. Opposites. So my idea for my dance theme is 'Fire and Water'. That's what everyone says about me and Ebyan, because we're so different, even though we've been best friends since nursery.

As soon as I get home, I log on to the dance music website that Miss Fizz told me about. For 'Fire' I choose a piece of music called 'Phoenix' by Geoffrey Keezer. It's a fast, dramatic piano solo that makes me feel lively and energetic. Perfect!

For 'Water' I find a tune called 'Rive Gauche' by David Michael and Gabriel Currington, which is much slower and full of passion. I find out on Google that 'Rive Gauche' is the left bank of the River Seine in Paris and a perfume by Yves Saint Laurent. All very French and romantic, like the music. *Très bon!*

I download the tunes and listen to both pieces over and over again on my iPod. I'm supposed to be counting out the beats and breaking up the music into sections so I can start thinking about the choreography, but I just close my eyes and let myself drift away. My body sways. I nod my head and tap my feet in time with the beat, rhythmically waving and wafting my hands through the air for 'water' and then slicing and cutting through it for 'fire'.

Diesel isn't too impressed at being left out. He rests his head in my lap and barks and barks until I plug my iPod into Dad's docking station and turn the music up loud so we can both bounce around the living room together.

Later that evening, at the studio, I play the music for Miss Fizz and she tells me to focus on the mood and tempo of the tunes and imagine myself dancing to each one. I picture a fast, fiery fusion of African, jazz and street dance for 'fire' and a slow, cool, calm, lyrical mix of modern and classical ballet for 'water'.

'Freestyle,' says Miss Fizz when I start dancing for real. 'Just dance. Do whatever feels right. Let your body lead you.'

I start with classical turned-out legs and pointed

feet, but she encourages me to experiment and put my own spin on the dance to show my style and personality. I dance a few steps with flexed feet and let my body form different shapes, twisting and turning and changing the pace and direction of the movements until my heart beats stronger and faster. I try out some high kicks, fast turns and big leaps. My spirit soars. I feel strong and powerful. I even throw in a couple of cartwheels and back-flips because I am so happy and excited.

'Bravo!' cries Miss Fizz, clapping with enthusiasm as if I have just danced the thirty-two *fouettés en tournant* from *Swan Lake*.

That's exactly how I feel too by the end of the class, and I collapse into a breathless, sweaty heap. Miss Fizz looks down at my battered body, but I know better than to expect any mercy.

'Remember the three Ds,' says Miss Fizz.

How could I forget? She's been drumming her 3-D motto into me three times a week for the last three years at least. *Discipline, dedication* and *determination* – the magic formula for every dancer who wants to reach their full potential.

'Kee-ee-eep dancing,' she says, impersonating the old guy on *Strictly Come Dancing*. She steps around my exhausted body and waves the street dancers into the studio. Most of them are girls, but for a moment I am distracted by one of the small group of boys.

He is tall and muscular, with spiky, sun-bleached blond hair and intense blue eyes, and he flashes a sympathetic smile at the sight of me slumped on the floor. I smile back, astonished. Sweaty puddle isn't a look most boys go for.

'I'll think about the transitions and connecting steps to blend your ideas together and make the dance less fragmented,' Miss Fizz is saying – and I yank my attention back to my dance.

8

Shopping

The next week, after my usual Saturday dance class, I go round to Suuqa Samiira to see Ebyan. The shop is full of Somali women talking fast and laughing, but Ebyan's mum spots me as soon as I walk through the door.

'*Assalaamu alaikum. Galab wanaagsan*, Keisha,' she sings out, greeting me in Arabic and then in Somali.

'*Alaikum wassalaam*,' I mumble, feeling self-conscious about my pronunciation and my sparkly black leggings. Everyone else is modestly covered up.

Mrs Warsame doesn't seem to care, and she hugs me warmly. 'Ebyan! Ebyan!' she calls – and my best friend's head pops round the changing-room curtain.

'Keesh! I'll be out in one minute – I need to finish this fitting.'

I wander up and down the rails of wedding clothes while I wait, gently running my fingers and my eyes over the light, colourful fabrics of the traditional Somali diracs and the shiny, silky white wedding gowns. In one corner of the shop, a henna artist is painting intricate patterns on the hands of a young bride and I stop to watch.

'If you're thinking of getting married, you need to find a boyfriend first,' whispers my best friend from behind me.

'Honestly, Eb,' I tease. 'Can't you think of anything else besides boys?'

'Shush!' warns Ebyan, glancing round to see if her mother is listening, but she is drinking tea and chatting with her friends.

'Don't worry,' I say. 'I haven't come to talk about boys. I've come to ask you a favour.'

'Anything,' says Ebyan. 'What do you need? Help with maths homework?'

'Help with dance costumes,' I say. 'Something light and flowing. I'm working on a piece about fire and water. I got the idea from what you said about your DT project. You know – the contrast between gold and silver.'

'Oh, I would love to help!' Ebyan responds, as I

knew she would. 'Fire and water? That's us!' She smiles, before rushing on. 'Are you performing in another festival? Do you have money? Let me ask Aba if we can go into town. I've discovered a great stall in the rag market.'

She charges off across the shop and I watch her clasping her hands together and pleading with her mother for the afternoon off. Mrs Warsame glances across the shop at me and then looks back down at her daughter to carry on the negotiations. I can't understand what she's saying, but when she reaches into the folds of her dress and pulls out two five-pound notes, I know she's agreed. That's the moment I also know I have to fess up and tell Ebyan the truth about why I need a new costume.

'It's not for a festival,' I say as we walk along the high road.

Ebyan blinks.

'It's for an audition,' I add quietly. 'I've applied for a Year Nine place at Birchwood School for Dance.'

Ebyan beams and points a finger at me. 'I knew you were up to something!' she says. 'That's brilliant!'

'Really?' I say. 'You don't mind?'

'Of course not,' says Ebyan. 'But why didn't you tell me?'

'I didn't want to talk about leaving and going to a new school when it might not even happen,' I say. 'But I've made it through the first stage, and now that I've got a second audition I'm starting to think my dream might actually come true.'

Ebyan loops her arm through mine and gives it a squeeze. 'That's the important thing, though, isn't it?' she says. 'Following your dreams? Trust me, if I had the chance to go to the College of Fashion, I'd take it without a backward glance.'

I gape at her.

'You only live up the road, Keesh,' she says, giggling at the look of horror that must be plastered across my face. 'It's not like we'd never see each other again. If you go to Birchwood, you'll still be able to come into the shop. I'll still be able to help you with your maths homework.'

I laugh. I pretend to wipe sweat from my forehead with my forearm and give a huge sigh of relief about the maths, but really it's because she's taken my news so well.

'Don't mention it to Destiny and Bee, though, will you?' I say anxiously.

'Not if you don't want me to,' says Ebyan. 'But why not?'

'I know they'd both be pleased and excited for me, but maybe a bit too much. Do you know what I mean?' I pause. 'Destiny will want to share the news with everyone on Facebook and Bee will want to shout about it and make a splash at school.'

'Isn't that a good thing?' says Ebyan.

'Yes, if everything works out,' I say. 'But if I fail – if I'm not accepted, it will be truly awful.'

'I don't like the idea of keeping secrets from our friends,' says Ebyan. 'But if you're sure it's what you want, I won't say anything.'

We catch the bus into town and get off right outside the Bull Ring. It's a huge, flashy shopping centre that looks like it could have flown in from outer space. But there have been markets here since the Middle Ages and the cloth – or rag – market was one of the first. It's an indoor market now and it sells loads of different stuff.

Ebyan drags me straight to Mushtaq Fabrics, which has rolls and rolls of sparkly, glittery material in every colour of the rainbow.

'Look at this,' she says, rummaging around and pulling out a length of shimmering greenish-blue barely-there fabric from the remnants basket. She wafts it about. 'Silk chiffon. I could make you a calf-length skirt to wear over your black unitard.'

Water. I can see it already – floating and swishing with my every move.

'Fire,' I say, dipping my own hand into the basket. I dig around until I find another piece of the same fabric – this time in a dazzling reddish orange. I hold it up against my leggings.

'Beautiful,' says Ebyan. 'That can be the top layer. We can use a giant hook and eye so you can slip out of it easily to reveal the bottom layer.'

'How much?' I say, looking at the stallholder.

Mr Mushtaq takes a frayed yellow tape from around his neck and quickly measures both pieces of fabric.

'Pah!' he says, glancing at me and then turning to Ebyan. 'It is not worth charging. For a beautiful girl and a regular customer like you, I will make this a gift.'

9

Blast from the Past

I rehearse until I know my dance back to front and inside out. It works. After a couple more private sessions with Miss Fizz, I have a good idea of what the finished piece will look like and I practise every day, on top of my regular dance classes, tweaking moves that don't click and improving my stage presence and acting skills. I want it to look relaxed and effortless on the outside, even though I know that on the inside my stomach will be bubbling like a witch's cauldron.

In my last session before the audition, I perform a full dress rehearsal in front of everyone from my dance class. They know about my Birchwood application and they understand the pressure I'm under. The class is only for serious dance students so most of them have been through the same sort of thing themselves

– entering competitions, auditions for shows, festival solos – and they are all rooting for me. But it feels weird that they know all about my audition while two of my closest friends still know nothing.

As I begin to dance, the first thing I notice is that I need to adjust my hairstyle. Mum has cornrowed my hair into an intricate pattern across my scalp to represent waves and flames and then plaited it with tiny blue and red beads. In my not-so-humble opinion, it looks amazing, but the beads keep lashing at my face and smacking me in the eye as I turn. It's a real shame, but I realize I will have to pull the plaits into a ponytail, pin them up and go back to being a traditional bun-head.

At the end of my performance, the other girls applaud and cheer loudly and Miss Fizz gives me some last-minute advice.

'Go home and have an early night,' she says. 'Don't go over the dance in your head, because without the music and your muscle memory, you'll just forget it and scare yourself stupid.'

I nod. 'Wish me luck.'

'Twiddle twaddle!' says Miss Fizz, laughing. 'You don't need luck. You're going to knock their socks off!' She becomes serious as she takes hold of both my shoulders and looks deep into my eyes. 'I know you can do it, Keisha. Just believe in yourself and dance from your heart.'

I go home feeling calm and confident, with Miss Fizz's encouraging and inspirational words ringing in my ears.

The next day, as I am stretching and warming up to perform the solo that might change my life for ever, I hear a high-pitched voice behind me.

'Keisha?'

I turn round.

'O! M! G!' says the owner of the voice. She says it exactly like that, spelling out the letters and leaving big pauses between them.

I stare. I'm pretty sure I've never set eyes on this girl in my life. She has long blonde hair twisted into three French plaits which are wound loosely around her head. She has rosy cheeks and a faint sheen of sweat on her upper lip, which makes me think she has just finished her audition and I wonder how her 'do' went down with the panel. Like my own first choice of hairstyle, it's not exactly a traditional ballet bun. Mind you, she is dressed in a puff-sleeved blouse, a twirly patchwork skirt and a pinafore, so perhaps she performed a character or folk dance – a Russian drobushki perhaps.

'It's me!' she squeals, breaking into my thoughts. 'Margot! Margot Dixon.'

Somewhere, at the back of my mind, the name *Margot* rings a faint bell, but I still can't place her. I guess I must have met her at some other ballet event – a festival, an exam or another audition – and I realize I am faced with a familiar and frustrating problem.

Nan reckons that when she was young, black dancers were so outnumbered by white dancers that loads of people recognized her just because of the colour of her skin, rather than her dancing. Sometimes, I think people remember me for the same reason and it's really embarrassing if I don't remember them back. I wonder if that is what's happening now, and I hope Margot Dixon isn't too upset when I have to admit that I don't have the foggiest idea who she is.

'Keisha?' says another voice behind me. 'Keisha Reid?'

I whirl round in a panic. Please! Not another blast from the past! I find myself face to face with Miss Pritchard, the ballet mistress I met at my first audition – and I sigh with relief. She smiles at me.

'Two minutes, Keisha,' she prompts. 'Are you ready? Do you have your music?'

'Y-yes,' I stutter, suddenly completely over-whelmed by nerves.

I rummage frantically through the mess of shoes, socks, leg-warmers, tights, hair bands, tissues, plasters, nail clippers, deodorant, toe tape, sewing kit, water, lip balm, compact mirror and cereal-bar crumbs in my holdall. My fingers finally fold around my iPod. I glance at Margot. I'm tempted to blame her for my loss of focus and concentration, but that would be a bit harsh. I know she's just being friendly.

'Good luck, Keisha!' she says enthusiastically, to prove the point – and then she hurries away.

'Thanks, Margot,' I mutter. 'You too!'

I hand my iPod to Miss Pritchard and I feel more fidgety than Diesel with fleas. She takes it from me with one hand and lightly rests the other on my shoulder.

'Calm down, Keisha,' she says quietly. 'Take some deep breaths. Count to ten and come into the studio when you're ready.'

I am teetering on the edge of a full-blown nervous breakdown, but I manage to do what she suggests.

I breathe. I count. And then I walk into the studio and stand in my starting pose. My knees are still wobbling, my hands are still trembling and I can hear my heart pounding so loudly I am afraid it might burst out of my chest.

But as soon as the music starts, I instantly forget all about Margot and Miss Pritchard. I forget everything and everybody around me, including the panel. Every last bit of stress and tension melts away. All I hear is the music. All I feel is my body moving and my feet dancing.

I am on fire! I begin with an energetic and hopefully impressive sequence of gravity-defying 'firebird' jumps. My skirt is a dazzling swirl of red and orange as I follow up with a complicated, but controlled combination of blazing ballet steps, scorching hip-hop moves and crackling acrobatics, building steadily to my finale. I gather my strength and energy and perform a huge *grand jété*. No one claps, of course – this is an audition, not a show dance – and as the last note fades, all that can be heard is the rhythmic hiss and puff of my breathing.

And then I am water. For the first eight counts, my body is frozen in a rigid, *demi-pointe* standing pose with my arms outstretched and my head turned to one side. I am perfectly quiet and still, except for the sound of my breath and the rise and fall of my chest. Then a slow, gentle ripple moves down my body from my head to my feet. The music washes over me and I move in the cool, calm, fluid way I have practised. Each graceful, lyrical turn is emphasized by the flowing blue-green swish of my skirt, and I finish with a precisely controlled flourish, sinking slowly to the floor into the splits.

I stand up and bow my head towards the panel, once more panting for breath, although this time it's totally for real. I'm not scared any more. I could do it again and again. I love dancing! From the top of my head to the tip of my toes, it makes me feel alive! My body expresses what I feel in the deepest part of my soul.

I feel free. I feel like me.

'Thank you, Keisha,' says Miss Pritchard. She presses the stop button on the music system and hands back my iPod.

That's it. No one else says a word. I have danced my heart out and hope that I have made sparks fly and caused a splash! There is nothing more I can do.

10

Flashback

On the bus home, Mum asks me a million questions about the audition. It's impossible to answer any of them. I feel as if I have just woken up and I'm struggling to remember a dream. Every time I snatch at a fleeting detail, it seems to disappear like a puff of smoke. And I am also uselessly racking my brains to remember where I might have met Margot before.

'Do you really not remember?' says Mum, when I mention her. 'You used to do baby ballet together. I was quite friendly with her mother.'

'Baby ballet?' I say. 'With Miss Fizz?'

'No, before that,' says Mum with a sigh. 'I used to take you to a different place in town.'

'What happened?' I ask. 'Why did you move me?'

'At your old ballet school, little kids were regularly

invited to take part in pantomimes and musicals, as well as ballets in local arts and community centres. You and Margot were part of a group of five little girls who went for an audition at the Alhambra,' she says. 'It's that enormous old theatre on the corner of Corporation Street and Ryder Street so it was a big deal.'

'I don't remember that,' I say.

'Yes, well,' says Mum, pressing her lips together. 'I went to quite a lot of trouble to help you forget.'

I stare at her, waiting for an explanation.

'It wasn't an open audition,' she says. 'You had all been pre-selected on the basis of age and height and how well you danced.'

'And?' I say, prompting her to go on.

'You were beside yourself with excitement,' she says. 'And I was so incredibly proud of you. It was your first time in a proper theatre and there we were, going through the stage door instead of the foyer. I always knew you were going to be a star.'

Mum's face crumples and I suddenly realize this is not a story with a happy ending. She rummages in her bag and finds a tissue. I really hope she's not going to start crying on the bus – but she delves into her bag again and takes out her purse. There is a transparent pocket for photographs, which is stuffed full of pictures of me and Dad. She prises them out and thumbs through them.

'Here,' she says finally, handing me a faded, dog-eared snap.

I stare at the picture. I am about three or four, standing in a line of other little girls with our arms slung around each other's shoulders and big grins on our faces. I look at our costumes – navy-blue leotards with spaghetti straps and a V-neck decorated with a pale pink bow, together with a pink satin underskirt, a navy net overskirt, pink ballet slippers and pink tights. All topped off with elasticated pink net cuffs on our upper arms and a navy velvet choker, with yet another pink bow. Super-cute!

I squint at the girl with the blonde curls, standing in the middle. I'm fairly certain it's Margot – and then, in a rush, the memories come flooding back to me and I see myself posing for the photograph as if it was only yesterday.

'Oh,' I say softly. 'I remember now . . .'

I have a flashback of myself standing on the Alhambra stage, gazing down into the orchestra pit and out at the stalls, and then up at the grand circle and upper circles, the gallery and the boxes.

There was a smiley lady who put on some music and asked us to dance around the stage to get used to it. Looking back, it was probably a good way to get us to warm up and give her an idea of what we could do. We skipped and twirled and remembered to smile like our ballet teacher had told us. Afterwards, the choreographer showed us a simple routine. When we had learned it and we were ready to perform, she called down into the stalls where the casting director was deep in conversation with the producer. He glanced up from his clipboard and his eyes briefly swept across the stage.

'Are you having a laugh?' he bellowed. 'Stop wasting my time! I'll take the three blonde ones.'

I was the only black girl there, but I remember it was the pretty, freckled, red-haired girl beside me who started wailing.

I hand the photograph back to Mum. It's brought difficult memories flooding back whether I like it or not. And it's made me realize how hard things have been for her as well, struggling to find the balance between supporting and encouraging me to follow my dreams – and protecting me from disappointment and heartbreak.

She's never been one of those pushy mothers, living

out her dreams of stardom through me. As a midwife, she's already a superstar to all those pregnant mums and new babies she helps. I don't know what to say to her now.

'Thanks, Mum' doesn't really seem to cover it.

I lean over and give her a big hug instead.

11

Bad Dreams

The following day, Ebyan and I are the first to arrive at our meeting place for the walk to school.

'How did you get on yesterday?' she says as soon as she sets eyes on me.

'Oh, Eb,' I say, slinging my arm round her shoulder and giving her a squeeze. 'The costumes you made for me were fab. Thank you so much. I think I—' I break off as I spot Bee and Destiny approaching. 'I'll tell you all about it later,' I mutter under my breath.

'I have to go straight home today,' says Ebyan. 'We've got relatives coming to stay for a few days.'

'No problem,' I say, trying to hide my disappointment. I really want to tell her about yesterday's audition, but I also need to talk to her about the Alhambra. Somehow I can't get it out of my mind. 'Maybe at the weekend.'

'The weekend?' says Bee, joining the conversation. She must have sharper hearing than Diesel. 'I've already got plans. The UK Indoor Athletics Championships. The club's hired a whole coach. A big gang of us are going to watch.'

I sometimes wonder what Bee sees in the athletics crowd. I think she gets hassled more than I do in ballet – only in reverse. Once, when I went to watch her compete for the Halsall Harriers, I actually overheard someone say she runs fast 'for a white girl'!

'What about you?' I say, looking at Destiny hopefully.

'Er ... I don't know yet,' she says, avoiding my gaze and looking like she can't think what to say to me. 'I, er ... I might get started on my food technology project.'

I immediately start to feel a bit paranoid. Did I hear right? I can't believe Destiny wants to stay in and do schoolwork instead of hanging out with me.

'Astonishing, isn't it?' says Ebyan, laughing and trying to lighten the mood.

'Don't look so shocked,' says Bee, joining in with the joke, but only adding to my sense of anxiety. 'We thought you liked surprises. That's what we thought you were working on when you didn't come in yesterday.'

Ebyan catches my eye again, but I bite my lip and don't say anything. I feel bad about not being honest with Destiny and Bee, and I'm sure they must suspect that something dodgy is going on. Maybe that's why Destiny doesn't want to hang out with me?

It's lucky I have my regular ballet class to look forward to on Saturday morning or I would end up home alone for the whole weekend. Still, it's not all bad, I think, trying to cheer myself up. I smile. Maybe I'll bump into that hot guy from the street-dance class again.

Everything is going wrong! On top of not finding out about my audition, I don't see the cute dancer again because when Saturday finally rolls round, my dance class is cancelled. Miss Fizz has a 'family emergency' – whatever that means – and the academy can't find a replacement.

I spend most of the day missing my cousin, and I actually end up thinking about my own DT project. The highlight of my evening is sitting down with Mum and Dad to watch *Strictly* on the telly!

I go to bed early and Diesel sneaks upstairs with me and lies on the end of my bed. I confide in him about how depressed and guilty I feel about keeping secrets from my friends. He looks at me sadly. He seems to be the only one who understands, but he can't offer any advice and I lie awake for ages, worrying and tossing and turning.

To distract myself, I imagine I am a prima ballerina, preparing to dance the lead role in *Swan Lake*. It's the story of a handsome prince and a beautiful princess who is trapped in the body of a swan by an evil sorcerer – and only true love can break the spell. The wizard's daughter impersonates the princess, tricks the prince and tries to steal him. Broken-hearted, the real princess flings herself off a cliff and falls to her death!

Odette, the white swan, is fragile and vulnerable and Odile, the black swan, is evil and manipulative so it's all a bit over-the-top and full of negative typecasting, but it *was* written in 1876.

Anyone who's seen Natalie Portman in the *Black Swan* film knows that playing two different characters is challenging and tough, but after weeks of rehearsals, I am ready. A prima ballerina, ready to dance Odette/Odile.

Opening night is here. I put the finishing touches to my make-up. From my backstage dressing room, I listen to the orchestra tuning their instruments, and over the tannoy I hear the stage manager's five-minute call to curtain time.

In the wings, I rub the soles and toes of my pointe shoes in the powdered resin tray so I don't slip, and I do a few last-minute stretches as I wait to make my entrance. I hear the quiet rustle of programmes and the buzz of conversation from the audience. There is a burst of applause for the conductor as she walks to the podium, followed by an expectant hush, broken only by an occasional cough before she raises her baton.

The lights dim, the curtain rises and the music begins. The first part – the prince at his birthday celebration – is over in a flash, and now a spotlight picks me out from the swirling mist of dry ice next to the moonlit lake and the audience gasps as they see my first delicate bourrée *and my expressive, fluttering* ports de bras.

I am flying without wings – and dancing like I've

never danced before. I feel myself bonding and connecting with the audience as I open myself up and pour my very soul into every aspect of my performance – from my pointed feet, high extensions and spinning turns to my balance and strength, and fluid adagio.

When I take my curtain calls, I receive a standing ovation and a stunning bouquet of exotic, perfumed flowers. I am whisked off to a glittering, glamorous party, and I know that tomorrow I will read the rave reviews of my performance in the Arts and Entertainments section of the morning papers.

Then suddenly everything changes. The music becomes scary and terrifying, like Tchaikovsky wailed by scalded cats.

As the evil wizard swishes his cloak and grimaces menacingly, instead of gliding gracefully across the stage I stumble and flail, unable to remember the steps. There are cruel jeers and ripples of raucous laughter from the audience. I am a double-dip dance disaster. I look more like a funky chicken than an elegant swan and to top it all off, someone in the corps de ballet kicks me really hard with a flying developpé à la seconde.

I feel as if I have been picked up by a hurricane

and hurled across the stage. I lie there, stunned and humiliated, as hot tears roll down my cheeks.

Someone calls my name . . .

'Keisha, sweetheart,' Dad says. 'You were having a bad dream.'

I open my eyes. I squint against the glare of my bedside lamp instead of the spotlight, and see him looking down at me. I struggle to sit up, wriggling myself free from the tangle of my duvet. The nightmarish images are already fading, but I am left with the feelings. Somehow, remembering what happened with the Alhambra casting director all those years ago has shaken me and I desperately wish I could talk it over with my friends. I feel nervy and on edge and my fears keeping popping up and jumping out at me.

I am afraid of not being good enough.

I am frightened of failing and of being rejected.

I am terrified of being judged on how I look instead of what I can do.

I am scared of how I will react if my dream of being a dancer is snatched away.

And worst of all, I am petrified that I am in danger

of losing my best friends and that it will all be my own fault.

'What are you so afraid of, Keisha?' says Dad, apparently reading my mind. 'What's going on?'

'I don't know,' I say, struggling to explain how I feel. 'Up till now, I thought I would get into Birchwood – or not – based on my dancing, and I believed I had the same chance as everyone else.'

'That's true,' says Dad. 'You do. You are a wonderful dancer, sweetheart, and for what it's worth, I think your worries and doubts are just the flip-side of confidence and belief.'

I stare at him in surprise.

'Nothing has changed except what's in your head,' says Dad. 'You have control over that. It's up to you how you look at things.'

Somewhere, deep down, I know he's right. I can't blame a chance meeting with Margot or an old photograph for how I feel. If I want my dreams to come true, I have to have faith in myself.

Dad brings me a glass of water and tucks me back into bed.

'Oh, I nearly forgot! After you went to bed, Béatrice phoned. She's having a party next weekend.'

Dad frowns as he tries to remember the rest of Bee's message. 'I think she said it's a slamper party – whatever that means.'

'Sleepover and pamper party,' I mumble with a smile, followed by a yawn.

12

Different for Boys

The next morning, I try to phone Bee to find out more about the party. Her mobile is switched off, so I try her home number.

'Ah, *je suis désolée*,' says her mum in her usual mix of French and English words with a Brummie accent. 'I am so sorry, Keisha. Béatrice is climbing rocks *avec ses frères* – with her brothers.'

'OK, no problem. Thanks, Mrs *Boo-shay*,' I say. 'I'll talk to her tomorrow at school.'

'Wait!' says Mrs Buchet. 'It is good you have called. You have heard about the *fête d'anniversaire* – the birthday party – *non*?'

Mrs Buchet is always a bit bossy, but she's leaving nothing to chance for Bee's birthday. She knows me and the girls want to buy presents for Bee, so now she gives me very precise details of what we should look for to match a present from her brothers.

'OK, no problem. Thanks Mrs Buchet,' I say again. 'We'll do our best.'

Next, I try Destiny, but she's not picking up, which I don't understand at all. We have always joked that we would have to be stone-cold dead – or at least in a coma – before we didn't take each other's calls. I call Ebyan and breathe a sigh of relief when she answers.

'I can't talk for long,' she warns. 'My aunt has gone into labour and we are waiting to hear from my uncle at the hospital. Oh, Keesh, it is *so* exciting!'

Talking about Bee's party and Ebyan's new baby cousin that's on the way remind me how much stuff is still happening that *isn't* to do with dancing, but like the true friend she is, Ebyan still wants to hear all about my audition. I finally get the chance to tell her about Margot too, and the story my mum told me.

'That's terrible,' says Ebyan. 'How can anyone choose a dancer just based on what they look like?'

'The worst thing is that it still happens,' I tell her. 'I know I don't look like some people's ideal image of a dancer – and it's not just because of the texture of my hair or the colour of my skin.'

'What do you mean?' says Ebyan.

70

'You know,' I say. 'For a start, I'm not a stick insect. I'm thin, but with curves. I have the three Bs – boobs, a belly and a bum.'

Ebyan laughs. 'Your ballet *bun* sticks out more than any of them!'

I dredge up a laugh of my own. 'The problem is, some people think dancers should all look the same, especially in the *corps de ballet*. In *Swan Lake*, for example, they reckon it doesn't look right to have a line of white swans with one or two black or brown ones in the middle.'

'That's ridiculous,' says Ebyan.

'I know,' I agree. 'In my opinion, the best ballet companies have a mix of black and white dancers.'

'If people don't think you fit in with the *corps de ballet*,' says Ebyan, 'you'll just have to take on the main roles instead.'

'Yes!' I say. 'Cinderella, Juliet, Giselle!'

'Seriously, though,' says Ebyan. 'Beauty isn't about everyone being the same. It can also be about difference.'

'It is different for *boys*,' I say. 'Carlos Acosta is a superstar and no one bats an eyelid over a black Romeo—'

'Sorry, Keesh, I have to go,' says Ebyan. She lowers

her voice to a whisper. 'Aba is nagging me to get off the phone.'

She hangs up abruptly and I make a decision. I've had enough of keeping secrets. Enough of telling lies.

It's time to tell my other friends about Birchwood. It's time to come clean.

13

Party Plans

First thing on Monday, like every morning these days, I sit next to the living-room window, chewing my fingernails and waiting for the postman to arrive. I know him so well by now that he knows I am waiting to hear from Birchwood and we've given each other nicknames. He calls me Patience, which he thinks is funny because I don't have any, and I call him Postman Pat, which I find vaguely amusing because his name really *is* Patrick. It would be even funnier if he had a red van and a black-and-white cat.

Last week, I threatened to set Diesel on him, but today he still turns up with junk mail and bills for Mum and Dad instead of a letter for me. And my dopey dog just rolls over and waits for Postman Pat to rub his belly. I find myself wondering if *Margot* has heard anything . . .

On the way to school, I try really hard to find the right moment to tell Bee and Destiny about my Birchwood application, but there doesn't seem to be one.

'Woo-hoo!' shrieks Ebyan as soon as she sees me. 'My uncle and aunty had their baby. I have a new baby cousin!'

'Girl or boy?' I ask.

'Boy!' she cries. 'His name is Guled. Honestly, Keesh – he's the cutest baby in the whole wide world!'

'Cute?' says Bee. 'If we're talking cute, you should have seen Mo Farah at the weekend – gorgeous as well as fast. It's a shame he's already married.'

'Did he win?' asks Ebyan.

'Of course,' says Bee. 'And thanks to me, he set another new five-thousand-metre indoor record.'

I laugh. 'Thanks to you? Why? Were you the pace-maker?'

'No, but trust me, I was shouting him on louder than anyone else in the whole arena,' she says. 'And you know what else?'

'He's leaving his wife and family so he can marry you,' suggests Destiny.

'Don't be daft,' says Bee. 'But he did high-five me

when he was doing his lap of honour.' She gazes at the palm of her hand and sighs. 'I may never wash again.'

Destiny laughs. She offers a Mini-Mint to everyone.

'What about you?' I ask her as I take one. 'I tried to call you. Don't tell me you really worked on your DT project the whole weekend.'

'Not the whole weekend,' she says, eyes shining and flicking towards Bee.

I can see it's the most I'm going to get out of her and I wonder if she's got something up her sleeve for Bee's birthday. On the other hand, I have a strong feeling that Bee knows more about Destiny's weekend than she is letting on, but has been sworn to secrecy. I suddenly have second thoughts about revealing my own secret.

'Guess what?' says Ebyan. 'Aba has agreed to let me go to Bee's birthday party. I got my uncle – Guled's father – to talk her into it.'

I'm impressed. Ebyan has spent nearly every Saturday since she was old enough to see over the counter helping out at her mum's shop, and now Mrs Warsame has let her have an afternoon off to come shopping with me and she's letting her come to Bee's party. Amazing! She must be really happy about that baby – and her uncle must be incredibly persuasive.

'That's great, Eb,' I say.

'We've got the full works,' says Bee, smiling broadly.

Her braces came off a few weeks ago so I'm not surprised she is taking every opportunity to show off her perfect pearly whites, alongside her glossy, shampoo-advert hair.

'It's not your birthday or anything, is it?' I say.

'Well done, Sherlock,' says Destiny.

Bee laughs and, as she looks away, I turn to Destiny and Ebyan and mouth 'present' at them. And just for a moment, I forget the letter that hasn't come. Forget the Alhambra and Margot Dixon and all my doubts. It's just me and my BFFs having a great time. And it feels fantastic!

14

Bee's Birthday

I'm the last to arrive at Bee's party and I'm totally knocked out. She wasn't kidding when she said we had the 'full works'. Her mum is so pleased that Bee has finally discovered her girlie side that she's gone completely over the top. The living room is decked out with pink, padded fold-up moon chairs, soft cushions and fluffy towels, silver and pink balloons and streamers. And there are four individual foot spas and a portable nail bar!

My friends are already wearing over-sized white towelling bathrobes and matching slippers, and their faces are smeared with green goo. They sweep me up into a BFF group hug, and after I change into my own robe, Bee applies my seaweed face mask. I begin to think some beauty-treatment bonding will be the perfect time for me to spill about Birchwood.

Mrs Buchet is usually a health-food freak, but she is clearly prepared to make an exception for birthdays. Instead of houmous with carrot and cucumber sticks, the dining table is weighed down with a pyramid-shaped wire stand stacked with fancy cup cakes, a chocolate fountain with marshmallow and fresh fruit dips, a popcorn maker, and all the fizzy, sugary ingredients for six different types of non-alcoholic cocktails, together with cone-shaped glasses, bendy straws, stirrers and cherries on sticks! It all looks totally delicious!

But the *pièce de résistance* is the awesome sight of Bee's three brothers filing into the room, dressed up as waiters. They are wearing black trousers and white shirts, which is basically the St Abadios RC High School uniform but with the addition of colour-coded bow ties!

'Lime for Lucas,' says Mrs Buchet, beaming at her sons with pride. 'Heliotrope for Hugo and—'

Heliotrope? I steal a quick glance at Hugo and see that what she means is purple – and then I do a double-take as I see the third brother coming into the room.

'And turquoise for Theo!' continues Mrs Buchet.

I can hardly believe my eyes. Bee's brother – Theo Buchet – is the mystery boy from Miss Fizz's street-dance class!

'Would you like a drink?' he says, smiling – and I have to wipe my clammy hands down the bathrobe before I can take hold of the list of cocktails he hands me to choose from.

I've never properly met Bee's brothers before because they're a bit older than us and they're usually away at the weekend doing some extreme sport or another – like rock-climbing, snow-boarding or free running. They are all bronzed and buff, but as I nervously watch Theo mix, shake and pour my *Caribbean Sea Breeze*, I'm in no doubt that he's my favourite.

Sadly, I don't think he even recognizes me under all the green gunk. He brings my drink, balanced on a little silver tray, and I reach out for it, but instead of focusing on the glass or looking into his dazzling blue eyes, I am staring down at the floor in embarrassment. Somehow, I knock the whole tray out of his hand, sending crushed ice, a dash of grenadine, equal measures of cranberry and pineapple juice and a sprig of mint crashing to the floor. Luckily, the glass is plastic so it doesn't shatter into a million pieces, but Theo's white shirt now looks as if it is splattered with blood.

I give a little yelp of alarm, shuffle backwards in my towelling slippers and trip over the hem of my towelling robe. I feel myself falling head over heels, but Theo reaches out and grabs me. He pulls me towards him, and for a brief moment he holds me in his arms and I lean into his mocktail-soaked chest – and once again, I am dissolving into a puddle.

'*Quelle horreur!*' exclaims Mrs Buchet, yanking me away from him. 'Are you OK?' For a nano-second, I think she is asking me, but her stricken expression is totally focused on her son. 'Let's get you out of those wet clothes and get that shirt into some bleach.'

She bundles him out of the room, closely followed by Hugo and Lucas, but just before he disappears from view, Theo glances back at me. He's still smiling and I sigh with relief.

The doorbell rings and the Buchet boys are almost immediately replaced by two professional Sparkle Spa beauty therapists.

'This was my dad's idea,' explains Bee quietly. 'He always goes over the top when he's feeling guilty.'

We all know Bee's parents got divorced recently

and her dad has gone back to live in France. Bee hasn't really forgiven him yet and I feel sorry for her.

The therapists set to work and we are treated to a *squeaky clean* facial, a *twinkle toes* pedicure and a *happy hands* manicure. A couple of hours later, when the therapists pack up and leave, we are so primped and preened and so stuffed full of cup cakes and cocktails, we can hardly move.

The living-room door opens again and Bee's family bursts back into the room. Her brothers have ditched the bow ties. Theo is now dressed in black jeans and a tight, dark green T-shirt – and he looks even cuter than before.

'*Bon anniversaire,*' says Mrs Buchet, holding up a pink-frosted birthday cake.

Bee's brothers start singing, and for a second we try to join in before we realize this is no ordinary rendition of 'Happy Birthday'. They have obviously been roped into it by Mrs Buchet and they look totally mortified, but they are doing the JLS version. I am so impressed, I gaze at Theo and I swear my heart actually misses a beat.

'*Mes frères,*' says Bee fondly when they are finished, and we clap and cheer and set off the party poppers.

Mrs Buchet has already given Bee some limited-edition GHD straighteners. Her brothers have clubbed together to buy their gift, and Hugo hands her a small parcel wrapped in pink wrapping paper, with purple ribbons. She tears it open to reveal a Cara silver link charm bracelet.

'Oh, wow!' she says, launching herself off the moon chair to give each of her brothers a hug. 'It's awesome.'

Next, we hand over our identical gift boxes and watch Bee's face as she opens the three tiny, matching Cara silver pendant charms that together form the slogan RUN – LIKE – A GIRL.

'These are so cool!' she yells, immediately realizing that the charms match the bracelet. 'How did you *know*?'

'Time to cut the cake!' announces Mrs Buchet, not giving any of us time to explain that it was her who bossed us about and got us all organized. She lights the candles and we burst into a second chorus of 'Happy Birthday'.

'Make a wish,' says Destiny as Bee sucks in a big breath and puffs out her cheeks.

She squeezes her eyes closed for a moment and then blows out all the candles at her first attempt.

None of us can eat another crumb, let alone manage a whole slice of cake, so Mrs Buchet says she will wrap a piece for us to take home tomorrow, and for the second time she and the boys leave us to it.

15

Truth or Dare

I'm sorry to see Theo leave again, but I'm happy to spend time with Bee and the girls.

'Let's play Truth or Dare,' suggests Ebyan.

I'm not that keen on the idea and I groan.

'Don't be such a grouch,' says Ebyan. 'You three have played it loads of times, but I've never had the chance before.'

'OK,' I say. 'Sorry, Eb. You're right. You go first.'

We start with a few dares. Ebyan sings everything she wants to say to the tune of 'Ten Green Bottles'. Bee savours the vomit-inducing taste of mayonnaise mixed with strawberry jam and I do an enthusiastic impression of a hen laying an egg. Bee turns up the pressure, daring Destiny to kiss a gnome and daring me to kiss a slimy, wart-covered, stone frog from the garden. Yuck! And then Ebyan performs a traditional Somali dance with so much booty bounce that I think she could teach Beyoncé a thing or two.

We move on to truth and reveal a few small, safe secrets. I admit that I am sometimes just a teensy bit afraid of the dark and Bee tells us about the most embarrassing moment of her life, which surprisingly is not the day she wet her knickers at nursery.

'I've got a boyfriend,' murmurs Destiny, while we are still howling with laughter – so quietly that I almost miss it.

'That's not news,' says Bee, still laughing – until she claps her hand over her mouth.

'It is to me,' I say, staring hard at my cousin.

'And me!' Ebyan adds.

I sense a subtle shift in everyone's mood, a slight tension in the atmosphere.

'Oh, Keesh, Eb,' Bee says, her face flaming. She begins to babble. 'I only knew because one of the Halsall Harriers lads is mates with Joel – they play football together – and he knows I know Destiny, so he was joking around and asked me if I'd be double-dating with them any time soon. And then

I said something to Destiny, and . . .' She tails off, and spins round to look at Destiny, waiting for her to say something more.

'I'm sorry, Keesh,' says Destiny. 'I was just too scared to tell you because I know you like him too. I've been seeing . . . Joel.'

'Joel Daley-Clarke?' I say stupidly.

Destiny nods.

'You're going out with him?'

'Not exactly *going out*,' she says. 'We didn't have our first proper date till we went to the cinema last Saturday to see the new Elliot Knight film.'

My face suddenly feels hot and my heart thumps madly. I really wanted to find out what Destiny was doing last weekend, but this is the last thing I expected. My eyes sting, but I manage to hold back my tears. For a second, I have no idea what to say. I feel hurt and angry, but how can I admit to that when I've been keeping secrets of my own?

'How long have you been seeing him then?' I ask instead.

'Since Valentine's Day,' she says. 'He gave me a card – no, he *made* me a card – with roses and a cello against a backdrop of sheet music.'

'Wow! How romantic,' I say. It comes out sounding

a bit sarcastic, but I am genuinely impressed. 'On Valentine's Day?'

'You weren't at school that day,' says Ebyan. 'Remember?'

I know what she's thinking. She's willing me on, prompting me to tell Destiny and Bee what I was doing on that day. I chew my lip. Now I know exactly how it feels when a friend keeps secrets from you – and I'm worried. I hope Destiny doesn't think I'm just taking revenge.

'OK,' I say, taking a deep breath and trying not to stumble over my words. 'I've got a confession. Remember when I told you I had a surprise? Well, it was more like a secret. A secret *I've* kept from *you*. I'm really sorry I haven't told you all before. I've applied for a place at Birchwood School for Dance, from next September. Valentine's Day was when I went for my first audition and I got a callback so I did a second one too – last week.'

Destiny's mouth drops open. Now it's her turn to be tongue-tied and stuck for words. Bee and Ebyan don't say anything either. The silence stretches out between us and I begin to wonder if my friends will ever forgive me.

'You knew?' Bee asks Ebyan eventually.

Ebyan lowers her eyes and looks at the floor, which is enough to let Destiny and Bee know it was my idea to keep quiet.

'I don't understand, Keesh,' says Destiny sadly. 'I didn't tell you about Joel because I didn't want to hurt you. But an audition? What's the problem? What did you think we would do – or say?'

I shrug and try to explain again about not wanting to push my luck by telling everyone about my application or talking to anyone at school about leaving in case I end up staying put.

'You still shouldn't have been going through everything all on your own,' Bee protests. 'We could have helped you. We could have supported you.'

'Exactly!' Ebyan agrees. 'That's what I said. You know you can rely on us. You know you can trust us.'

'Sharing dreams!' adds Destiny, getting up and coming across to give me a hug. 'That's what best friends – and favourite cousins – are *for*.'

'You're right,' I say, hugging her back. 'But what about boys? What are they for?'

'Sheesh, Keesh!' says Ebyan. 'Even I know that.'

'Do we need to spell it out?' asks Bee.

I glance at my friends and laugh, before looking back at my cousin.

'It's cool,' I tell her. 'I'm really glad you and Joel are together. But you could have told me, you know. There's no way we could ever fall out over a boy.'

'Or over dance,' says Destiny.

16

Street Dance

I catch my first sight of Destiny and Joel together after school on Monday. They're strolling down the high road arm in arm, whispering to each other as if it's the most normal thing in the world. But it's not normal. It's weird. Usually, Destiny would be walking home with me and Ebyan and Bee. My heart starts pounding and my face feels hot.

But I'm not jealous, I realize. I truly am happy for them both – though I also feel a bit embarrassed. Back in the day, I used to think that Joel Daley-Clarke was all that and a bag of chips! I liked him ever since we started high school, and up till now, he was the only lad I've ever had a crush on. Bet he knew it too! I backed off when I realized that Destiny liked him as well and I always thought she had done the same.

From then on, I was happy to admire him from afar, although that didn't stop me sitting behind him in ICT, gazing at the cute peppercorn curls on the back of his neck – and daydreaming about him.

'Are you OK, Keesh?' asks Ebyan, interrupting my thoughts.

'Yes, sorry,' I tell her. 'I was miles away.'

'You're not thinking about Joel, are you?' says Bee.

'Yes,' I admit, 'but not like that. I can't really think about boyfriends right now anyway. I'm too busy thinking about Birchwood.'

'Good!' says Ebyan.

'Besides,' I add, grinning at them both, 'he's not the only boy in the world! I've—' I bite my tongue. I don't want to say too much in front of Bee!

Now that my audition is over, I don't have my extra Monday evening practice session with Miss Fizz and I'm already getting withdrawal symptoms. I change out of my school uniform and pull on an old, baggy tracksuit and look through my collection of dance DVDs. We've seen them all so many times that Mum and Dad refuse to watch them any more, but they won't be home from work for ages so I slot the classic

Step Up into the DVD player. After a few minutes, though, I turn it off and grab my iPod instead.

I have to move! I need to shake off all my anxieties – waiting to hear from Birchwood, seeing Destiny and Joel together, my DT project . . . I need to dance!

I leave a quick note for Mum and catch the bus to the Kennedy Academy. Most of the studios are already in use, but Miss Fizz hasn't arrived yet and her room is empty. I know it won't last so I don't even bother to change out of my tracksuit into my leotard or swap my trainers for ballet shoes. I quickly connect my iPod to the sound system and scroll through the playlist until I find the *Streetdance* movie soundtrack rather than one of my usual classical ballet or audition tunes.

I stand in front of the wall of mirrors and study my reflection. I pull off my hairband, shake out my hair and close my eyes for a moment. Instead of my practice routine at the ballet *barre*, I warm up my whole body, focusing on each major muscle group, starting at my neck and shoulders and gradually working my way down towards my toes. I pull up through the centre of my body to maintain my posture and keep my back flat as I stretch my legs in split and hurdle positions and alternate between pointed and flexed feet.

When my temperature is raised and I can feel the blood rushing through my veins, I peel off my tracksuit top. And then I just let myself go.

The music takes over and carries me away. I bend and fold and twist and turn. I flick and kick. I stretch and slide, and push and pull. I leap and spin. I don't stop until the music fades to silence – which is shattered by a sudden burst of applause.

My head snaps up and I open my eyes. The street-dance class are gathered in the doorway, waiting to get into the studio. They have been watching me. Theo is amongst them and my heart leaps. And when he smiles, my heart soars. I think he likes me.

'I really hope you haven't been dancing in my studio with outdoor shoes,' rings out Miss Fizz's voice from somewhere in the middle of the group.

I glance down guiltily, gather up my belongings, stuff them into my bag and make a dash for the door.

'Not bad,' says one of the street-dance boys as they all pile into the studio. 'If you're going to join us, though, you'll have to learn the difference between your whacking and your krumping.'

I'm still smiling when I get home. Mum and Dad are in the kitchen, preparing dinner – and so deep in conversation that they don't notice me come in.

'Of course, I'm incredibly proud of her,' Mum is saying, 'but that second audition was really competitive – even amongst the parents. Some of those yummy mummies are really pushy.'

Dad laughs. 'You're a yummy mummy,' he says. 'And anyway, Keisha's chances don't depend on how pushy you are or whether you know the French word for *pirouette*.'

I nearly laugh out loud myself and give myself away.

'Devon,' says Mum, 'that *is* a French word.'

'I know,' says Dad. 'Give me some credit. It was a joke.'

'It's the fees that are the real joke,' says Mum, suddenly serious. 'Even if Keisha is offered a place, there's no way we can afford to pay them. She needs to be offered a full Dance Scheme scholarship – and they are as rare as hens' teeth!'

'You're right,' says Dad gloomily. 'I can't bear the idea of her being disappointed. I'm scared.'

I'm scared too. I drop my bag on the hall floor.

They hear the noise and turn round.

'Oh!' says Dad, taken by surprise. 'Hello, Keisha. I didn't hear you come in. I didn't know you were home.'

'Hello, love,' says Mum. 'How long have you been standing there?'

'Long enough,' I say.

'Sweetheart,' says Dad, crossing the kitchen to hug me. 'I'm so sorry. Money is really tight, but I didn't want you to find out like that.'

'Don't worry,' says Mum. 'I'm sure you'll get a scholarship.'

'But what if I don't?' I ask.

'If you don't . . .' Mum's voice wobbles and trails off into silence.

Dad takes a deep breath. 'If you don't,' he says, 'you won't be able to go to Birchwood.'

My heart stops beating. My blood runs cold.

17

Evening News

The next couple of days pass in a blurry mix of stress and anxiety about Birchwood, scholarships and my DT project – and just when I think my life can't get any worse – it does!

Out of the blue, I bump into Margot Dixon on the way back from ballet class.

'O! M! G!' she shrieks. 'I heard from Birchwood! I've been offered a reserve place!'

'A reserve place?' I echo, parrot-fashion. 'What does that mean?'

'The letter says . . . hang on, let me read it.' I wait, in stunned silence, while she rummages in her bag and then reads it aloud. '*We will, however, be pleased to offer you a reserve place in the event of the with-*

drawal of one of the girls awarded a place in the lower school.'

I still don't really get it. Why is she so excited? She'll only get a place if someone else drops out, which everyone knows hardly ever happens. But what I do understand is that I don't have my own letter from Birchwood. I obviously haven't been offered any sort of place at all!

Suddenly, all my dance dreams come crashing down and shatter into a million pieces around my feet. There has to be some mistake, I think. But I know there isn't. My head spins and I feel dizzy. I can't bear to listen to listen to Margot's misplaced, triumphant glee any more.

'That's great, Margot,' I manage. 'Congratulations. I have to get off now. Mum will be expecting me.'

'Fingers crossed.' Margot beams. 'It would be great if we both get in – so much easier to settle if we already have a friend.'

I walk home quickly, fighting back my tears. Mum's home, but I shout through to her that I want to do my homework before dinner and I race up to the safety of my room so she won't start asking me questions. I text my friends:

Birchwood turnd me dwn. I nd u.

For the next twenty minutes or so, I lie on my bed with a huge lump in my throat, staring at my phone. No one replies and I am suddenly scared. What if they are still fed up with me after all? My life is a full-blown disaster zone! Then the doorbell rings.

'Keisha!' Mum yells up the stairs. 'It's for you.'

I barely have enough time to scrape myself up off my bed before Destiny, Ebyan and Bee burst into my room.

'Got your text,' says Bee, skinning her teeth. 'We've come to cheer you up.'

'And to offer you the benefit of our superior wisdom and advice,' says Ebyan.

Destiny launches herself across the room and hugs me – really hard and tight.

I am so relieved to see them it's an effort not to burst into tears or throw myself at her feet in gratitude.

Destiny's mobile rings and she glances at the screen and cuts off the call. 'Joel,' she says. 'But he won't mind. He'd never try to come between me and my friends.'

'I always liked him,' I say, adding quickly, 'but like I said, it's OK – I don't any more.'

'Why?' says Destiny. 'What's wrong with him?'

'Nothing! I don't mean like that,' I say, dredging up a smile. 'I just mean I don't fancy him like I used to.'

'She's got her eye on someone else,' says Bee – and I flinch. I wonder if she has guessed that it's her brother, Theo.

'*Make new friends, but keep the old,*' quotes Ebyan. '*Boyfriends are silver, best friends are gold.*'

The mention of silver and gold reminds me of the audition costumes she made for me, and my disappointment must be written all over my face.

Destiny slides her arm back round my shoulder. 'Let's have a look at the letter then.'

'What letter?' I ask.

'How much snail mail do you actually get?' says Bee. 'The letter from Birchwood, of course – or did they email you? Don't tell us they let you know by text!'

'Oh, I haven't heard from them yet,' I say.

My friends all look at me like I have lost my mind, and for a second or two no one speaks.

'So how do you know you haven't been accepted?' says Ebyan.

'Margot Dix—' I begin, then stop.

How *do* I know I haven't been accepted? I slap my palm against my forehead to knock some sense into myself as I suddenly realize that I *don't*!

'You got us round here under false pretences,' jokes Bee when I finish telling them about Margot Dixon and her 'reserve place'.

I try to stay positive and hope that my letter will arrive, but the next morning, Postman Pat arrives empty-handed again, except for another pile of junk mail.

'Why aren't you answering your phone?' Bee asks as we walk to school.

'What do you mean?' I say. 'Have you been trying to call me?'

I take my mobile out of my bag and see that I've somehow managed to put it on silent. There are texts from Bee, Destiny and Ebyan – and a couple of unanswered calls from a number I don't recognize.

I hold it up to show her. 'Was this you?'

'Er . . . not exactly,' says Bee with a mischievous smile.

I feel a rush of heat to my face. She doesn't need to say anything else. She knows! It's Theo.

Theo's been ringing me!

18

Dream Date

On Sunday afternoon, Theo turns up on the doorstep with two bikes – his own and the one he has borrowed from Bee for me.

'Hi, Keisha,' he says. He leans down and brushes his lips against my cheek so gently that I can hardly feel it, but his breath is minty fresh and he hasn't gone over the top with the Lynx. 'You ready?'

'You should have warned me,' I say, glancing down at my short, lacy dress and then back at the bikes. 'I'm not really dressed for cycling.'

'Sorry,' he says, his blue eyes twinkling. 'We can leave the bikes, if you like.'

'No,' I tell him, grinning back. 'It's fine. Just give me a minute to get changed.'

It's ages since I've ridden a bike – but isn't it

meant to be one of those things you never forget? I hope that's true. I race back into the house and up the stairs. In my room, I dither about what to wear and worry that Theo will get fed up with waiting and leave before I am ready. Eventually, I decide on my black skinny jeans and red canvas lace-ups.

When I go back outside, Dad is standing on the front doorstep talking to Theo. For a second, I think he might be doing his protective father bit and I'm mortified, but they are getting along like old mates and Dad can hardly wait to wave us off. He obviously thinks a date is just what I need to cheer me up and distract me from thinking about Birchwood.

We cycle to Cannon Hill Park and then along the track that runs next to the River Rea. Theo leads the way and I wobble along behind him. The trail is totally flat, but when he notices that I am struggling to keep up, he pedals madly away into the distance, teasing me, before doubling back to wait and let me catch up.

I know from Bee that all her brothers are sporty and very competitive. As well as street dance and cycling, Theo likes free running and rock-climbing, but I can see he has a soft, gentle side too.

We chain the bikes to the park railings and wander

through the Centenary Plantation woods. The ground is carpeted with bluebells, gently dancing in the breeze.

'Still no word from Birchwood, then?' asks Theo.

I bite my lip. 'Not yet,' I tell him. 'I'm not holding my breath, though. Not any more.'

'From what I saw of your dancing last week, you're bound to get in,' he says.

'That wasn't real dancing,' I protest. 'I was just messing about.'

'You're only saying that because it wasn't ballet,' says Theo. 'It looked real to me – and the rest of the street-dance class. That's how we dance all the time.'

He tucks a stray braid behind my ear, leans closer, cups my face in his hands and gently kisses me. His lips are soft and dry and warm. A shiver runs down my spine and my insides melt and turn to mush. It's my first proper kiss. I feel my face flush and struggle to hold his gaze. Those big, blue eyes seem to see right inside of me.

'Let's dance!' says Theo, breaking the tension.

I glance around and feel a stab of panic. 'What? Here?'

Theo laughs. 'If you like,' he says. 'But I know somewhere better.'

He takes my hand and sets off at a run, steering me through the trees and flowers and out of the woods. We keep going and he pulls me after him, past the playground and tennis courts, the crumbling Golden Lion building and the boating lake, until we reach the bandstand.

The last time I saw this place, the wooden roof was crumbling, the cast-iron supports were rusting and it was covered with scaffolding, but it's been restored. There's a string quartet sitting playing in the middle of it and a handful of mainly older couples waltzing around the paved dance floor that circles them.

'They do this nearly every Sunday,' says Theo, laughing and pulling me amongst them. 'If there's no band, they bring a CD player.'

I recognize the music. It's 'The Waltz of the Flowers' from *The Nutcracker* by Tchaikovsky, but I've never danced to it like this before. Theo takes me in a proper ballroom hold and guides me round, twirling and spinning me until I am dizzy – and then he folds me into his arms and we just sort of sway together. The music fills my head and seeps deep down into my soul. I want this moment to last for ever, but when the musicians take a break and head off towards the Garden Tea Rooms, we decide to cycle home.

It's almost dark by the time we arrive.

'Thanks, Theo,' I say. 'That was awesome. I had a really great time.'

'Me too,' he says, blue eyes twinkling. 'Would you like to go out again some time?'

Oh, I would, I would!

He kisses me again – quickly, on the cheek, since we've both spotted Dad peeping round the curtains. I smile as Theo walks away, wheeling the bikes on either side of him.

'*Au revoir, ma chérie*,' he calls over his shoulder. He is half French, after all.

19

Dance Dreams

First thing Monday morning, I phone Birchwood. It was Nan's idea. She Skyped me to get an update. She reckons our 'mailman' must have been abducted by aliens – and she thinks it's better to find out the result of my audition once and for all.

It takes me ages to psych myself up. My heart is pounding and my breath is coming in short, shallow bursts. Anyone would think I had been dancing.

'I was just wondering if you could let me know what's happening with my application,' I say to the administrator, thinking of Margot Dixon and explaining that I know at least one person who has already received a letter.

'You're right, Miss Reid,' says Mr Price. 'Most of

the places for next year have been allocated, although some applicants may be offered a place later if anyone withdraws or drops out.'

I feel my heart plummet. 'So does that mean I haven't even got a reserve place?'

'Did you apply for a scholarship?' he asks.

'Yes,' I say. 'Does that make a difference?'

'Oh, yes, yes, yes,' says Mr Price. 'The final decisions regarding the Music and Dance Scheme scholarships were only made on Friday and the remaining letters were put in the post then. I'm sure yours must have been amongst them.'

'So can't you just tell me the result now, over the phone?'

'Oh, no, no, no,' he says – about a million times – just in case I didn't get it the first time. 'That's strictly against Birchwood School for Dance rules. I'm sure the letter will arrive later today – or perhaps tomorrow.'

I put the phone down with a sigh.

'Don't give up hope, love,' says Mum as I leave for school.

Later, I sit in history, trying – and failing – to concentrate on whatever Mr Khan is saying about

110

the causes of the Second World War. Out of the corner of my eye, I spot a woman hurtling across the playground, frantically waving what looks like a small white flag above her head. It's the universal sign of surrender, but there's no one else in sight. She's moving so fast I wonder if she's one of Bee's athlete friends who has lost her sense of direction on the way to the Alexander Stadium and ended up here by mistake!

As the woman comes closer, though, I blink in astonishment and turn to look out of the window properly.

'Keisha Reid,' says Mr Khan. 'How many times do I—?'

He stops abruptly as he follows my line of vision, drawing the attention of the whole class to the woman in the playground. It isn't a confused runner – and she's not waving a flag. She's waving an envelope.

'Oh, no!' cries Destiny from the desk next to me. 'Is that . . . ? What's she doing here?'

I groan and bury my face in my hands. Unfortunately, Destiny is right. It's her Aunty Esme – *my* mum! And if I had to take a wild guess, I'd say she has brought my letter from Birchwood. I am torn. On the one hand, I am desperate to know the news, but couldn't she have waited until I got home from school like any normal mother?

I part my fingers and watch in horror as Mum peers through the glass and waves when she spots me. She sets off at a run again towards the main entrance and a moment later, she bursts through the classroom door. How she got past the office, I don't know, and if our headteacher – Mrs Parveen – catches sight of her, she'll go nuts!

'Excuse me, madam,' says Mr Khan. 'I don't know who you are or what you want, but I must ask you to leave.'

'I'm Keisha Reid's mother,' announces Mum, waving the envelope under Mr Khan's nose and trying hard to catch her breath. 'I'm so sorry to disturb you, but I've brought her Birchwood audition results.'

'Birchwood?' says Mr Khan. He's the sort of teacher who always uses ten long words when one short one would do, so his question is a bit of a surprise.

'Yes,' says Mum. 'Birchwood School for Dance. I opened the envelope by mistake, and she's been waiting for ages and it didn't seem fair not to bring her the news immediately.'

By mistake? Yeah, right. If I know Mum, she probably steamed it open!

Mr Khan hesitates. He seems to have doubts too. He looks around the classroom at the sea of curious, waiting faces. He looks as if he would be nearly as happy as me if I get into Birchwood. At least then he would never have to deal with my crazy mother ever again!

'Please endeavour to undertake the task expeditiously,' he says. 'If Mrs Parveen detects your unauthorized presence on school premises, my position – or possibly my life – will be terminated.'

Mum gapes at him as if he's speaking Martian.

'Make it snappy,' translates Destiny helpfully. 'If Mrs Parveen catches you here, he's a dead man!'

I walk to the front of the classroom and Mum hands me the envelope. I glance back at Destiny, and then at Ebyan and Bee. They put their hands up and cross their fingers for me.

Surely it's good news. Mum wouldn't have run all the way here to break my heart in front of everyone. And the envelope feels thick. That's a good sign too. Surely a rejection letter would be a single sheet of paper in a much smaller envelope?

I look down at it. There's no doubt that it's from Birchwood. The school address is printed across the top above my own. Here at last, in black and white,

in the palm of my shaking, sweating hands, is the
answer to my dreams – or the most crushing news
of my entire life.

'Please, Keisha,' prompts Mum. 'Read it.'

20

Best Friends

I take a deep, ragged breath and pull out the wad of papers inside. An expectant hush falls over the room as my eyes skim down the top page. I look up at Mum, at Mr Khan, at my best friends and the rest of my class.

'I'm in!' I tell them – and suddenly I can't stop grinning. Life can't get better than this! 'And I've got a full scholarship. *I'm going to study ballet at Birchwood School for Dance!*'

Mum flings her arms round me, and Destiny, Ebyan and Bee race across the classroom to join us in a group hug, screeching and squealing and jumping up and down on the spot.

'Brilliant!' says Destiny. 'I'm so proud of you.'

'*Life leads us to different places, but friendship*

115

always remains,' says Ebyan, who always has a perfect poetic quote for every occasion. 'Congratulations, Keisha.'

'*Félicitations, ma copine*,' says Bee, which is French for roughly the same thing.

As she hugs me, I spot Joel Daley-Clarke leading a burst of applause. He claps and cheers and stamps his feet and the whole class joins in.

'Perhaps we could postpone the celebrations until we adjourn for break,' says Mr Khan. 'Please, all of you, be seated.'

Mrs Parveen storms into the room – and I seriously fear for Mr Khan's life.

'What is all this racket?' she demands. 'Who is responsible for starting this . . . this riot?'

We scuttle back to our desks, leaving Mr Khan and Mum to explain.

Mrs Parveen manages a tight smile when she hears the news, but she is quick to escort Mum out of the classroom and encourage everyone else back to work.

I sigh happily – and I definitely can't focus on the dates Mr Khan is writing on the board. Woo-hoo! I'm going to be a ballerina!

My dance dreams have come true!

Destiny

That was months ago, and quite a lot of exciting things have happened since then. In the summer holidays, Nan came to visit us from New York. She took me and Keisha shopping in London and to see the new *Ballet Black* production at the Royal Opera House.

Keisha started Year Nine at Birchwood in September. She found it tough at first because she was really missing Diesel and me – and the rest of her friends and family.

We're all still really close, but it's hard for us to get together because Keisha has to be at school by ten past eight every morning, including Saturdays, and sometimes she doesn't get home till seven in the evening! It's a good job Miss Fizz drummed the three Ds into her for all those years – dedication, determination and . . . er, something else that I can't remember. But it's Keisha's dream and I'm really happy for her.

Oh, and I'm still going out with Joel and he's the best boyfriend ever.

Ebyan

Keisha and I have been at the same school, in the same class, since we were three! I had the Easter break, the whole summer term and the summer holidays to get used to the idea and it's only a few weeks since she started at Birchwood, but I already miss seeing her every day.

Since I made her 'fire and water' costume, though, Miss Fizz and lots of students from the Isabelle Kennedy Academy of Dance have asked me to make their costumes too. I am such a regular customer at Mushtaq Fabrics that the stallholder gives me special discount rates all the time now.

Watching Keisha fight so hard to achieve her dreams has made me think seriously about what I want to do with my own life. I have decided I don't want to follow in my mother's footsteps and take over the family business. I don't want to sell clothes any more, even if they are wedding dresses. I want to design and make them. I haven't told her yet – I'm hoping Uncle Abdi will help me. It's the sort of thing that can break a mother's heart, but Aba is tough and strong. And I know she'll support me.

Bee
The new outdoor athletics season started soon after my birthday. At school events, nothing much changed – I'm running against girls in the same year

group, as always. But the Halsall Harriers fixtures are a different matter. I moved up from the under-thirteen age category to the under-fifteens and I'm feeling the pressure. I'm competing against girls who are older, bigger, stronger and more experienced than me and it's really tough. Sometimes I line up in the starting blocks and I already know I'm going to come last. My reputation as an under-thirteen record-breaker counts for nothing with the older athletes, but at the same time the Halsall Harriers middle-distance coach has high hopes and huge expectations of me.

There have been a few moments when I have thought about giving up and trying ribbon-twirling or maybe knitting instead. *Maman* would probably be happy – but my brothers just tell me to get a grip and focus on my goal of reaching the next Olympics. They reckon that whatever the older girls say out loud, inside they are worried that their reputations are at risk from a young *upstart* like me. I know they're right. I may not be able to catch the older girls just yet, but I will soon be breathing down their necks. All I have to do is stay positive and run!

And Keisha? All she has to do is stay positive and dance – and not get too distracted by my brother!

She's been seeing Theo for ages. They think it's all hush-hush and pretend to be 'just getting to know each other', but I've seen that mushy look in their eyes.

Keisha

Ballet is brutal! But as everyone keeps telling me, if it was easy, it would be called football. I used to think I would die if I didn't dance, but I'm beginning to think it is dance that will kill me. All the stories Nan and Miss Fizz ever told me about the blood, sweat and tears are totally true.

I've only been at Birchwood a short while and already I've learned loads, but I am totally exhausted. I have spent hours and hours practising the same exercises over and over again in the studio and at the *barre*, striving for perfection.

At first, I felt as if the 'old girls' were all staring at me and judging me. But I've made a few friends now, including Margot, who finally got a confirmed place – O! M! G! – *and* turned out to be really nice.

As well as ballet, I do jazz and contemporary, and I'm also really busy with history and English and all the usual subjects – so Ebyan still gets to help with my maths homework and give me style and fashion advice.

Destiny still gets to help with my hair and make-up and give me food and nutritional advice.

Bee still gets to help with health and fitness and give me . . . well, lately she's been giving me boyfriend and dating advice!

And me? I'm just trying to hang onto my friends and follow my dreams. Right now, I'm working so hard I don't have lots of time to spend with my BFFs, but I know they are there for me, and they know I am there for them too. Life is leading us down different paths, but whatever happens we are always going to be friends.

For ever!

Acknowledgements

I would like to thank . . .

My BFF, Edwina, for always being there and always knowing the right thing to say and do;

My sons, Garikai and Dan, for their love, inspiration and advice – plus help with my blog, social media platforms and website: www.malaikarosestanley.com;

My family, friends and writing buddies for their generous encouragement and support;

My agent, Catherine Pellegrino, for being the best;

My cover illustrator extraordinaire, Sarah Coleman aka Inky Mole;

And last, but most definitely not least, everyone at Tamarind Books/Random House, for all their hard work in bringing this *Sugar and Spice* book to fruition, especially Ruth Knowles, Parul Bavishi, Kirsten Armstrong, Sue Cook, Laura Bird and Harriet Venn – and Tamarind founder, Verna Wilkins.

Music Previews

www.dancefestivalmusic.co.uk/ballet-dance-music-32/intermediate-ballet-music-35/rive-gauche-170.html

www.dancefestivalmusic.co.uk/ballet-dance-music-32/intermediate-ballet-music-35/phoenix-109.html

http://youtu.be/bQA5Fnher3o

About the author

Malaika Rose Stanley grew up in Birmingham. She has worked as a teacher in Zambia, Uganda, Germany, Switzerland and Britain. She is now a full-time writer and the Royal Literary Fund Fellow at the London College of Fashion. She also runs creativity and writing workshops for children and adults. Her publications for Tamarind include *Spike and Ali Enson*, *Spike in Space* and *Skin Deep*.

Malaika enjoys travel, singing, reading, ballet and football. She lives in North London near her grown-up sons.

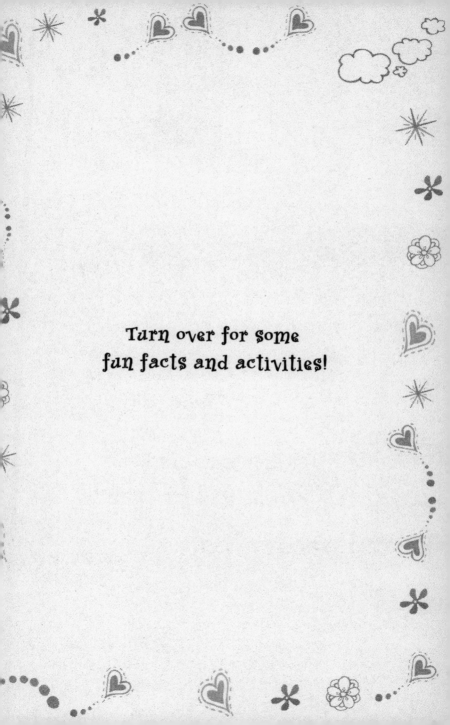

Turn over for some
fun facts and activities!

Follow your dance dreams!

'The myth was that because you were black you could not do classical dance. I proved that to be wrong.'
Arthur Mitchell

In 1969, Arthur Mitchell and Karel Shook founded the Dance Theater of Harlem in New York.

'Ballet is a tough career choice. If you truly want to make it, you must have dedication and determination. You might be the only black student in the class, but keep your head down and get on with the job in hand – maybe you will be inspiring the next generation to follow in your footsteps.' Cassa Pancho

In 2001, Cassa Pancho founded Ballet Black in London.

Fabulous facts about ballet

Tutu is a French word, changed from *cucu*, which is a baby-talk version of *cul*, meaning 'bottom' or 'backside'. But in Hawaii, tutu means 'grandmother', in New Zealand it's a poisonous plant, and in Brazil, Tutu de Feijão is a paste made of beans and manioc flour!

People tend to think of a tutu as the whole ballet dress, but really it is just the skirt section and the bodice is made separately. A tutu starts life as ten metres of net in strips of varying stiffness.

Pointe shoes have a box to support the dancer's foot while she is dancing on her tiptoes. This helps to create the illusion that she is floating weightlessly. A busy professional dancer can get through up to six pairs of *pointe* shoes a week.

Ballet dancers have to be elite standard athletes as well as artists. They need to be able to move fast and jump high. They need to sustain a performance over an extended period with bursts of explosive energy like a footballer, but with the elegance of a gymnast or ice-skater.

Dance anagrams

Can you solve these anagrams?

Famous ballets:

1. truant checker
2. ankle saw
3. cleaner lid
4. true moon jailed
5. buying a steeple

Films about dancing:

6. set pup
7. creased tent
8. grand city din
9. yo hen
10. bank claws
11. kettle ahead
12. party methods
13. sable hotels
14. whale candles?
15. detest avalanches

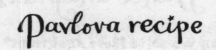

Pavlova recipe

Pavlova is a dessert created and named in honour of the famous Russian ballerina, Anna Pavlova, after one of her tours to Australia and New Zealand in the 1920s.

Ingredients

- 3 large egg whites
- 175g castor sugar
- 275ml double or whipping cream
- Fresh fruit, for decoration

Method

1. Beat the egg whites with a hand whisk or in a food mixer (not a processor) until you have soft white peaks, but don't over-whisk or the mixture will collapse.

2. Gradually add the sugar, whisking after each spoonful until the mixture is thick and glossy.

3. Line a tray with baking paper and spoon the meringue into a 20cm circular mound with a hollow in the centre.

4. Bake in the centre of the oven at gas mark 2, 150°C or 300°F for 60 minutes. Turn off the heat and leave (overnight) in the oven to cool.

5. Serve topped with whipped fresh cream or cream mixed with an equal quantity of plain yoghurt, and decorate with fresh fruit – strawberries, kiwis, mangoes, bananas and sliced preserved ginger . . . nom, nom!

Bee's birthday
mocktail recipes

Caribbean Sea Breeze
Crushed ice, a dash of grenadine, equal measures of cranberry and pineapple juice and a sprig of mint

Yellow Bird
Crushed ice, equal measures of orange, pineapple and grapefruit juice, fizzy lemonade and a twist of orange

Pomolo
Vanilla ice-cream, topped up with cola

Piña Colada
Crushed ice, 3 measures of pineapple juice, 1 measure of coconut cream

Spring Fling
Crushed ice, 1 measure of lemonade, 2 measures of cranberry juice, dash of soda water, cherry

Apple Fizz
Crushed ice, 3 measures of apple juice, 2 measures of lemonade, dash of lemon juice, sprig of mint

Sugar and Spice quiz

What kind of friend are you?

1. I am...

a) enthusiastic and emotional

b) clever and confident

c) caring and creative

d) responsible and reliable

2. My friends think I am...

a) funny and up for a laugh

b) determined and up for a challenge

c) energetic and up for adventure

d) easy-going and up for trying new things

3. When I talk to other people I am...

a) chatty and often change my opinion

b) decisive and make up my mind quickly

c) sensitive to other people's point of view

d) good at listening and interested in other people's ideas

4. People like me because I am...

a) dramatic and friendly

b) realistic and practical

c) artistic and helpful

d) sympathetic and generous

5. My best qualities are my...

a) leadership and passion

b) ambition and confidence

c) imagination and concern for others

d) relaxed attitude and flexibility

6. When I plan things I like to...

a) decide what I want at the time

b) sort things out in detail and in advance

c) make group decisions

d) let other people decide

7. When things need to get done I like to...

a) work in a team and be in charge

b) do it myself to make sure it's done right

c) discuss new ways of doing things

d) share ideas and make sure everyone is happy

8. My life motto is...

a) keep smiling

b) do it now

c) reach for the stars

d) go with the flow

9. I am full of...

a) life

b) confidence

c) ideas

d) patience

10. I would like to be less...

a) messy

b) bossy

c) moody

d) lazy

Mostly As: Miss/Mr Popularity

You like other people and you make friends easily

You are always up for new things and are the life and soul of any party

You are creative and colourful

You don't hold grudges and you apologize quickly

Mostly Bs: Miss/Mr Independent

You are self-sufficient and don't need to lean on your friends

You like to be right – and you usually are

You are very confident and focused on your goals

You are a born leader and organizer and you work well in groups

Mostly Cs: Miss/Mr Creativity

You make friends slowly and carefully but you are very loyal and reliable

You don't really like being the centre of attention

You are talented and creative and may be musical and/or artistic

You are a good listener and you care for other people

Mostly Ds: Miss/Mr Adaptability

You get on well with other people and you have lots of friends

You are easy-going and relaxed

You are sympathetic and kind

You are a good listener and you are able to sort out problems

Also available in the Sugar and Spice series:

When thirteen-year-old Destiny enters the Bright Sparks beauty contest behind her (ex-model) mum's back, she is determined to prove she has talent and brains – and that she is not just a pretty face.

Together with her cousin, Keisha, and best friends, Ebyan and Bee, Destiny deals with every challenge life throws at her – including scary eyeball-to-eyeball confrontations with bully-girl Bella and secret winks from heart-throb, Joel.

And then real disaster strikes . . .